PETE FOR PRESIDENT!

by Daisy Alberto
illustrated by Blanche Sims

Kane Press, Inc.
New York

For the Alberto and the Ramirez families—D.A.

Library of Congress Cataloging-in-Publication Data

Alberto, Daisy.
  Pete for president! / by Daisy Alberto ; illustrated by Blanche Sims.
     p. cm. — (Social Studies connects)
  "Civics - grades: 1-3."
  Summary: Best friends compete with each other for third grade class president.
    ISBN 1-57565-142-4 (pbk. : alk. paper)
  [1. Schools—Fiction. 2. Best friends—Fiction. 3. Friendship—Fiction. 4. Elections—Fiction. 5. Politics, Practical—Fiction.] I. Sims, Blanche, ill. II. Title. III. Series.
   PZ7.A3217Pe 2004
   [Fic]—dc22

                                             2003024180

10 9 8 7 6 5 4 3

First published in the United States of America in 2004 by Kane Press, Inc.
Printed in Hong Kong.

Social Studies Connects is a registered trademark of Kane Press, Inc.

Book Design/Art Direction: Edward Miller

www.kanepress.com

Joey and I are best friends. We have known each other almost since we were born.

We've always done everything together—sort of.

When we were babies, Joey crawled first. But I crawled faster.

Joey walked first. But I walked farther.

Joey talked first. But I talked louder.

Now we are in the third grade.

"Listen up, class," says Ms. Grant. "At the end of next week we will have class elections. Who would like to run for president?"

GRADE 3
CLASS ELECTIONS
NEXT WEEK!

Did You Know?
In lots of countries, people don't get to choose their leaders in elections the way Americans do. Americans are lucky!

I think about it.
Presidents get to fly in their own
special airplanes.

AIR FORCE ONE

Presidents get to live in the White House.

Presidents get to throw out the first pitch of the baseball season.

Well, maybe not the president of Grade 3, but it still sounds like fun! And hey, you have to start somewhere.

Did You Know?

The first time a U.S. president opened the baseball season was in 1910—almost 100 years ago! That president, William Howard Taft, was a big baseball fan.

I look at Joey. He looks at me. Joey raises his hand first. I raise mine higher. "I'LL DO IT!" we say at the same time.

"Not so fast," says Ms. Grant. "First someone has to nominate you."

"I nominate Joey," I say.

"I nominate Pete," says Joey.

"May the best candidate win!" says Ms. Grant.

Joey and I grin. "I will!" we both say.

A person who runs for a job in an election is called a **candidate**. People **nominate** a candidate. That means they suggest someone for the job.

After school, I make a poster. I'm almost done
when my marker runs out. I finish with chalk.

The next day, Joey has posters—big, fancy ones with stars. Joey looks at my poster. "Who is Pet?" he asks. Mike and Joey laugh.

Oh, no! The e at the end of my name is smudged. You can hardly see it. My campaign is off to a bad start.

A **campaign** is everything a candidate does to get votes—from giving speeches and making posters to building websites and doing TV commercials.

I get home from school and flop down on the living room floor. "You're blocking the TV!" yells my brother, Dave.

Dave is watching a movie about a guy who wants to be mayor of an Old West town. He gives people stuff so they'll vote for him—and makes promises, even when he knows he can't keep them.

In the end, the sheriff puts the guy in jail.

But I don't pay attention to that part. I'm too busy thinking about how I'm going to be president of Grade 3! "Watch out, Joey!"

Did You Know?

When James Polk ran for president in 1844, he promised to make Texas a state. He won the election—and kept his promise!

The next day at lunch, I sit next to Max. Max loves pizza. "Vote for me, and I'll make sure our class trip is to a pizza factory!" I say.

"Grrmpurlmph," says Max. His mouth is full, but I think that's a "yes."

I dribble up to Myra at recess. "Vote for me," I say, "and for the class trip, we'll go to a basketball game."

"I'll think about it," she says.

I find Erika in the library. "I don't think we need a class trip," I tell her. "Vote for me and we'll use the money we save to buy computer games."

Zap! beeps Erika's computer. "Maybe," she says.

The next day Joey has a big box of doughnuts on his desk. Chocolate. My favorite. I reach out to take one. "Hands off!" Joey says.

Max walks up.

"Vote for me," says Joey. "Have a doughnut!"

If you like doughnuts, vote for Joey!

I watch as the whole class gobbles up the doughnuts. "That's not a balanced breakfast," I grumble. No one pays attention.

Joey gives me a chocolatey smile. Uh-oh. I have a feeling he may have seen that movie, too.

The next morning, I hang up a new poster. It has a picture of Joey on a kangaroo's body. Mike laughs when he sees it.

"Vote for me, and you can be class monitor," I tell him.

"Great!" Mike says.

Joey goes home for lunch. When he comes back, he has a new poster. It's a picture of me from last Halloween. I'm dressed as a clown. "Hey!" I say. "No fair!"

"You started it!" says Joey.

"No name calling," says Ms. Grant. She makes us take the posters down.

For the rest of the day, Joey doesn't talk to me. And I don't talk to Joey. "Remember," says Ms. Grant just before the bell rings, "the debate is tomorrow."

"Good luck," snarls Joey. "You'll need it."

"I'm not worried," I say. But I am.

Did You Know?

The first presidential TV debates took place in 1960 between Richard M. Nixon and John F. Kennedy. In a **debate**, people give reasons for or against something.

On the day of the debate, Joey and I stand in front of the class. Joey glares at me. I glare right back. "Why should you be president of Grade 3?" Ms. Grant asks me.

That's easy! "Because I'm the best candidate."

"Ha!" Joey says. "You still sleep with a nightlight!"

I can't believe he said that. This is war! "So?" I say. "You sleep with a teddy bear!"

"Nightlight baby!" says Joey.

"Teddy bear baby!" I say.

"Am not! Are too!" we both yell.

"STOP IT!" someone shouts. Joey and I stop.

"What about the issues?" Erika asks. "What are your platforms?"

Huh? Joey looks at me, and I look at Joey. Issues? Platforms?

Erika rolls her eyes. "I mean, what will you do for Grade 3? What do you stand for?"

"Where do you stand on the class trip?" someone calls out.

Did You Know?

In 1912, when Teddy Roosevelt was running for president, his platform said that women should be allowed to vote. A **platform** is all the things a candidate promises to do if he or she is elected.

"You told me we'd go to a pizza factory," says Max.

"You told me we'd go to a basketball game," says Myra.

"If I were president," says Erika, "I'd let everyone vote on the class trip. And I'd work for better food in the cafeteria. And no tests on Fridays!"

Everyone starts talking at once. "Vote for Erika!" someone yells.

"But Erika's not even running," says Joey. "You can't vote for her."

Ms. Grant stands up. "Actually, they can," she says. "She can be a write-in candidate."

Oops. Joey and I didn't know that.

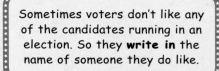

Sometimes voters don't like any of the candidates running in an election. So they **write in** the name of someone they do like.

The next day is the election. When it's time to vote, I check my name. Then I cross it out. I write ERIKA on the ballot instead.

Ms. Grant counts the votes. Erika's the new president of Room 3!

JOEY PETE ERIKA

BALLOT BOX

One way to vote is to mark a piece of paper called a ballot. Here is Pete's ballot.

President
☐ Joey
☑ Pete
ERIKA

Joey and I take down our posters. It's nice to be doing something together again.

"Erika will be a good president," Joey says.

"Yeah," I say. "The best person won."

JOEY'S THE MAN FOR THE JOB

Joey and I ride our bikes home after school.
"Friends?" says Joey.
"Friends," I say.
Joey grins first. But I grin wider. I know we're both thinking the same thing . . . .

There's always next year!

I can make thoughtful decisions!

MAKING CONNECTIONS

Elections involve a lot of decision making! You have to choose which candidates to nominate and then vote for the candidate you think will do the best job. It's a big responsibility!

Look Back

Pete starts his campaign on page 12. What does he do? Look at pages 16–17. How does Pete try to convince his classmates to vote for him? Does it work? Look at pages 23–25. How does the debate change the outcome of the election? Why does Pete decide to vote for Erika?

Try This!

Write your own platform!
Look at Erika's platform on page 26. If you were class president, what would you do for your class? Think about the important issues in your classroom, and decide what *you* stand for!